M
Manor
Mystery

BY

LISA TRUMBAUER

ILLUSTRATED BY

KEVIN HAWKES

For my mother, Sigrid Trutkoff,
who went to the Mountain House with me — L.T.

For information contact:
MONDO Publishing
980 Avenue of the Americas
New York, NY 10018
Visit our web site at http://www.mondopub.com

Printed in USA
06 07 08 09 10 11   9 8 7 6 5 4 3 2 1
ISBN 1-59034-810-9

Designed by Jean Cohn

Library of Congress Cataloging-in-Publication Data
Trumbauer, Lisa, 1963-   Mountain manor mystery / by Lisa Trumbauer ;
illustrated by Kevin Hawkes.   p. cm.   Summary: During a family vacation
at an old mountain resort, ten-year-old Ben and his new friend Trina uncov-
er a mystery involving a pair of stolen candlesticks and a missing writer of
children's books. ISBN 1-59034-810-9 (pbk.) [1. Hotels, motels, etc.—
Fiction. 2. Authors—Fiction. 3. Mystery and detective stories.] I. Hawkes,
Kevin, ill. II. Title.   PZ7.T7845Mou 2006   [Fic]—dc22   2005008129

Contents

CHAPTER 1   *Welcome to the Haunted Manor* 4

CHAPTER 2   *What Are You Doing Here?* 12

CHAPTER 3   *That's Him!* 19

CHAPTER 4   *A Little History* 26

CHAPTER 5   *The Saga Begins* 34

CHAPTER 6   *Oh, Henry!* 40

CHAPTER 7   *Lowell and Behold* 47

CHAPTER 8   *A Family Affair* 54

CHAPTER 9   *Maybe I Took Them* 60

CHAPTER 10   *A Picture Is Worth a Thousand Words* 67

CHAPTER 11   *Could It Be?* 73

CHAPTER 12   *Nowhere to Be Found* 79

CHAPTER 13   *Napkin Scribbles* 83

CHAPTER 14   *Open to the Public* 90

Welcome to the Haunted Manor

I knew Mom and Dad had big plans for our summer vacation. I just hadn't realized that those plans involved staying in a hotel that resembled a haunted house from an old Dracula movie.

What could they have been thinking? Family bonding, that's what!

It all began the evening of the last day of school, after I had thrown away all my old school papers, and my sister, Carrie, had gabbed on the phone for hours with all her friends. Mom and Dad had pulled Carrie and me into the dining room for a family discussion, determined that we would sit and listen and then agree with whatever important decision they had arrived at.

We hadn't had a family discussion in, like, eons.

You see, Mom and Dad had both been away a lot on business trips throughout most of the winter and spring. Not at the same time. Sometimes it would be Dad traveling around and other times Mom who was away. I'm not really sure exactly what my parents do. Every time we have career day and kids are asked to invite their parents to come and talk about their jobs, my parents always decline, saying their jobs are too complicated to explain.

Of course, that doesn't help me understand what they do

any better. I know Dad works for some big company in New York City. Every morning he gets up much earlier than Carrie and me and drives to the station to catch the train to New York. Then in the evening, Dad walks in the door at about seven-thirty, totally exhausted but usually relieved to be home. It sounds like a grueling and long day, but when I asked my parents why Dad doesn't just work here in town—I've seen plenty of offices here—they pretty much just patted me on the head and said that Dad had a good job in New York and that the family couldn't afford for him to change his job right now.

So I still don't know what that job is.

Mom, on the other hand, works in town. She says she's an artist who works on computers. I'm not sure how it's done, but she designs things with a special program. I'm good with computer games and surfing the Internet, but I don't know much about complicated computer stuff. Mom's a whiz at it, and she travels sometimes to show people what she can do. This past spring, she traveled way more than usual.

Which leads me to where we are now—about to go on a family vacation, doing some family bonding, which Mom and Dad said we seriously needed. Usually for our family vacation, we stay at a hotel down on the shore and do beachy stuff—nothing out of the ordinary. We usually vacation with other families so Carrie and I have friends to hang out with.

Not this year. This year, Mom and Dad decided it would be just us Cantrells. Bonding.

Before we left, Mom and Dad showed us a brochure of our vacation destination.

"It's a great resort in the Catskill Mountains," they said, anxious for us to climb on board their idea of a terrific time.

6

"Carrie and Ben—you're going to love it!"

Now, when I heard "resort," I imagined a huge swimming pool, a high-tech game room, perhaps a beach nearby, maybe even a boardwalk. The word "resort" sounds like a place that should be by the ocean, doesn't it? It also sounds like it should come with a lot of upscale stuff, like a TV and a DVD player—you know, everyday modern amenities.

Nope, no modern amenities here!

Of course, being in the mountains of New York, we're not near the ocean. I'm not that much of a dunce that I didn't realize that. I just had a different picture in my head of a "resort." Instead, this is what I saw as we turned every which way up the mountain:

First, I saw a bunch of gardens off to one side.

Next, I saw a few gazebos under some leafy trees. (What's the purpose of a gazebo, anyway?)

And then finally, I saw it—our hotel. It loomed up out of the mountains, like an ancient decrepit castle from one of those old black-and-white horror movies you can sometimes find on late-night TV, complete with a million windows and balconies and stone arches, even a few turrets. Although it was daytime, my imagination conjured up a ghostly mist, swirling around the base of the hotel, and bare branches of trees, reaching their skeletal fingers up to the sky.

In actuality, the trees were leafy and green and the sky was a pure blue.

Perhaps my imagination was on overdrive because the hotel looked so dark and menacing, like the home of a crazy scientist conducting secret experiments on dead bodies. New hotels always seem to shine in the sunlight, don't they? Maybe it's the paint or the cement that they're made from that give them the sparkly appearance of new construction.

But this hotel was dark and dreary—dark stone, dark iron balconies, dark trees stretching beyond the rooftop.

Totally creepy.

I guess its name is perfect for it—the Mountain Manor House. After all, it is in the mountains, and it definitely resembled a big old manor or a huge mansion, but not a house. I thought, though, that a better name for the place would be the *Haunted* Manor House, because I reasoned a ghost or two must have been lurking around somewhere.

I could tell that Carrie wasn't too thrilled with the Mountain Manor House either.

"What *is* this place?" she moaned next to me in the backseat of the car as we pulled up to the front entrance of the hotel under a really tall stone archway, just ripe for cobwebs to grace the corners.

"Isn't it wonderful?" Mom exclaimed. "It's so old and full of history."

"It's full of something, all right," Carrie continued. "But I'm not sure it's anything I want to see."

"You'll love it," Dad said as he got out of the car. "It has a lake and rowboats and hiking trails—"

"Hiking trails? Rowboats? What is this—summer camp?" (That was Carrie again.)

We all got out of the car. "The Cantrell family is getting back to nature," Dad explained as he began unloading luggage from the back of our car. I decided to help and keep quiet. Carrie could do enough whining for the both of us and express the horror we were both experiencing. She's always been more of a talker than me.

"That's right," Carrie said with a roll of her eyes. "I forgot. No modern-day distractions so we can do some family bonding."

"Correct!" Mom chimed in gleefully, placing a flowered bag on the luggage cart that a uniformed teenager wheeled over. "We were all too caught up in our own things this past year. This week we're going to get to know each other again."

Mom and Dad were so excited, I didn't have the heart to point out that Carrie and I would never "bond." Once, maybe, we were pretty close—as close as brothers and sisters can be, I suppose. But ever since Carrie entered middle school two years ago she's acted like she's way better than the rest of us. She most definitely could not be bothered with her "baby" brother.

I'm so not looking forward to when she enters high school.

And now I had to spend a whole week with her in a hotel room. With no TV. It was beyond my comprehension that the fates had landed me in such a predicament.

Apparently, it was beyond Carrie's, too.

Mom and Dad had decided that Carrie and I would share a room. During past vacations, I usually stayed with Dad, while Carrie stayed with Mom. I guess we were now old enough that we could be trusted on our own.

Not a lucky break for me.

As soon as we checked in, Carrie began rampaging around the room like this vacation was all my fault, muttering under her breath about the unfairness of it all, and shoving clothes into drawers, then taking up all the hangers in the closet.

I decided to leave all my stuff in my suitcase.

After a few minutes of twiddling my thumbs—literally—I was itching to press the button on a TV remote control. I couldn't listen to Carrie anymore, so I told Mom and Dad I was going exploring.

"Don't forget, we have to be in the dining room at seven for dinner," Mom reminded me.

How *could* I forget? Dinner at the Haunted Manor House was a swanky affair, meaning everyone had to get dressed up. Men had to wear suits, and if I had been 15, I would have had to wear one, too. And there was no grabbing a hamburger or a slice of pizza on the sly. Nope. Four-course dinners, whatever a "course" was. I guessed I'd find out soon enough.

I grabbed my digital camera that Dad had sent me for my birthday, and I left Carrie to our room and her griping. I say "sent" because Dad was out of town on business for my big day—my tenth birthday. I'm not even sure where he was. Chicago? San Francisco? Some big city west of New Jersey, which is where we live.

Anyway, I was expecting a phone call from him, when instead I got an overnight package. Inside was a digital camera, with instructions for how to view the first few pictures. And there was Dad, holding up a sign that said, "Happy Birthday, Ben!" and then another picture of Dad sitting in front of a huge ice-cream sundae with a candle in it.

Okay, it was kinda dorky. But it meant a lot to me anyway, as did the digital camera. Unlike cameras with film, you can delete pictures on a digital camera. I kept the ones of Dad.

But back to our vacation at the Haunted Manor House.

I strolled through the hotel, taking pictures with my digital camera, becoming totally engrossed in the spooky atmosphere of the place. The hotel really was very old. The dark floors were wooden, with faded flowered carpets over them, and they creaked when you stepped in certain places. The hallways were narrow and sort of dark, and they turned into other corridors that seemed to wander off to nowhere. In the middle of the hotel was this really cool wooden staircase that went up, up, up, complete with squeaky stairs and all. Our rooms were on the second floor, so when I got to the staircase, I knew that one floor down was the lobby, with a few large dining rooms and other places called "common" areas. Not very exciting. So how about if I went up, up, up?

I climbed the wooden steps, imagining that my camera was an old flickering candle lighting my way. By the time I got to the top—the tenth floor—I was a little winded, but I was also clicking pictures like mad. I don't think I'm a pro-photographer or anything, but the staircase had all these really cool angles, and I was shooting them from different heights.

Well, it was something to do, at least.

At first, I thought the tenth floor would be just like our hallway, and it was, sort of. The tenth floor had lots of doors with numbers on them, which were probably hotel rooms, just like ours.

I wondered if any of them had someone like Carrie inside.

But when I reached the end of the hall, I came to a door that had a sign on it, just begging someone to turn the knob. The sign read, "Do Not Enter."

How could I resist?

"If it's locked, I won't be able to go in," I said to myself. "But if it's *unlocked…*" (You can finish the rest.)

And what do you know? That old glass doorknob turned in my hand.

I pushed the door open and went inside.

CHAPTER 2

What Are You Doing Here?

Okay, I know I shouldn't have gone in. My parents would have told me that a sign that clearly states "Do Not Enter" has been put there for a reason. But "Do Not Enter" sounded like an invitation to me, especially since the door was unlocked. I mean, if the hotel staff didn't want anyone to enter, they should have locked it, right?

So I went inside. I didn't need to turn on a light, because the room was positioned in the corner of the hotel, which meant it had two really large windows on two walls, allowing the sun to shine through brightly. I don't know what I was expecting the room to look like, but it looked, well, kind of ordinary.

I already said it had two large windows. The windows actually went from the floor all the way up to the ceiling, and from where I stood, I thought I could see handles on those windows, at the sides. So that meant that the windows were probably doors that went out to a balcony. The windows were covered by lacy white curtains, and on each side of the windows hung these long red drapes. Blood red.

In one corner of the room, set at an angle, was a large, old desk, slightly battered and used looking. A chair sat in the very corner, facing into the room, and the desk stretched from one wall to the other, forming a triangle. I saw one of those desk blotter things on top of the desk and what looked like a very old pen set. Two pens stood erect, and a little pot waited on the right, like it still might contain ink. A couple of candlesticks completed the desk's landscape, but the long, skinny candles you usually see in them were missing.

To my left was a wall full of books, which looked really ancient and dusty, some with cracked leather bindings and faded yellow pages. On the wall facing me, between the bookshelves and the desk, was a huge portrait of a man sitting at a desk. In fact, he could have been sitting at the desk in this very room. He wasn't very old. I'm not good with adult ages, but he looked like he was younger than my parents, so I guessed he was maybe in his twenties. He was holding a pen and writing in a notebook.

Maybe the pen was the same as one of the ones on the desk, I thought. *Cool!*

I moved farther inside the room and looked behind me. A couple of chairs stood against the wall near the door. The chairs were a faded gold color, almost like mustard, with a really fine diamond pattern etched into the fabric. The material appeared very fragile; I was afraid if I sat on one, it would tear. Wooden legs sprouted from their seats, and when I looked closer, I noticed that the arms of the chairs had been carved to resemble the paws of an animal. On closer inspection, the legs of the chairs looked like an animal's legs, too, like the legs of a lion maybe.

I began taking pictures of the room. Snap—I captured the desk and chair. Snap—the man in the picture. Snap—the bookshelves and all the books. I walked across the room and leaned in close to the desk. Snap—the pen set and the desk blotter. Snap—the candlesticks. Snap—a view outside the windows. I turned around to take a picture of the yellow chairs. Snap—

"Hey! What are you doing here?"

As I was snapping, a girl entered the room. I was so surprised to see her in my camera's viewfinder, that I almost dropped my camera.

Living with Carrie, I'd learned that the best way to answer a question from a girl was with another question. "What are *you* doing here?" I countered.

"Um, I was just looking around," she admitted, suddenly looking guilty.

I felt bad for making her feel that way. "Yeah, I'm looking around, too. Do you know what this room is?"

"Nope. My family just checked in. My parents were taking care of my baby sister, so I thought I'd take a walk."

Now, I didn't know what kind of "baby" she was talking about, but Carrie called me her "baby" brother. So right away, I became defensive. "Baby, huh? How old?"

"Oh, I don't know anymore. Eight—"

"Eight! She's not a baby if she's eight!" I defended.

"She is too a baby!" the girl shot right back. "She's not even a year old."

Realizing she meant eight months, not eight years, I felt like a total dweeb. "Sorry," I mumbled. Not wanting to feel like a dweeb, I stood taller and introduced myself. "I'm Ben. My family drove in today from Jersey."

"Hi!" The girl offered me a big smile. "I'm Trina. We came in from Connecticut."

Okay, I've started noticing girls a little bit, so I could say

and mean it that Trina looked all right. Her dark brown eyes were wide and interesting, and her smile was warm and not too big or scary. She even had a few freckles, and she was about as tall as me. She wore white shorts with a pink T-shirt, making her look very summer-vacationy.

"What do you think of this place?" I asked her.

"This room, or the whole hotel?"

"Both."

"I think the hotel's kinda cool, although I wish we had a TV. I'm going to miss a whole week of my favorite show."

"Yeah, the TV thing is a bummer."

"But the lake looks pretty cool," she said. "Have you seen the lake?"

"Lake?"

"And there are all these lookouts around the lake and up the mountain. Have you seen those?"

Huh?

"And how about the gift shop and the ice-cream parlor?"

I didn't know what she was talking about. "All I've seen is my room and the staircase and this room," I told her.

"Well, have I got a lot to show you!"

Now, I was thinking, "You do?" It seemed like Trina thought she was going to pal around with me, at least for the next few hours. I was thinking about how to tell her that I wasn't really looking for a pal, when someone else entered the room.

"What are you doing here?"

Trina and I both nearly jumped, startled out of our sneakers. We turned around, and standing in the doorway was this very old woman, dressed in overalls, a white shirt, and a long, dark green jacket. She had on a big straw hat and worn-out brown hiking boots, and she was leaning on a wooden walking stick. I wouldn't call it a cane. Canes are smooth and have a curved top. This thing was a gnarled, old stick, with bumps all over it. The woman's gray frizzy hair stuck out from the sides of her hat as if it were being smushed down and pushed outward. She looked like a gardener or someone who worked outside, not someone who would be walking up ten flights of wooden steps to get to this musty, old room.

"Um, w-w-we were just looking around," I stammered.

"Didn't you see the sign?"

"What sign?" Trina asked. (She probably hadn't seen it, because I had left the door open.)

"The door was unlocked," I jumped in.

"Unlocked, hmm?" the old woman said skeptically.

"Most of the rooms in the hotel are open to guests," Trina spoke up. I didn't know if this was true or not, but it sounded true coming from Trina. I was beginning to discover that Trina was very good at speaking up.

"Well, this room isn't!" the old woman fairly barked, lifting her stick and bringing it down sharply for emphasis as she took a few steps away from the door and closer to us. The thump was like the sound your shoe makes when you kick it off while you're lying on your bed and it falls to the floor.

Trina and I instantly backed up and tried to scoot around her, but she raised her arms at that moment, as if casting a spell.

"You kids stay out of here!" she said again, shaking those arms, walking stick and all.

"Y-yes, ma'am," I stuttered.

"We didn't hurt anything," Trina added.

"Doesn't matter," the old woman growled. "This room is off limits. Off limits! This hotel has plenty of places for you to play. Now go on—skedaddle!"

Skedaddle? Play?

Trina and I didn't hesitate. We flew around the old woman and took off down the hall, nearly tripping down several flights of steps on our way. On about the fifth floor we stopped and started cracking up.

"Who *was* that old lady?" Trina laughed, holding her side.

"I have no idea. But she seemed really mad."

"I hope we don't run into her again."

"I'm with you on that."

"Well, I'd better go," Trina said. "This is my floor. It's almost time for dinner."

"Dinner!" I said, smacking myself on the forehead. "I've got to go, too, then."

"See ya around, Ben from Jersey!" Trina shouted with a wave as she dashed down the hall.

"See ya!" I shouted after her as I dashed down the stairs to the second floor.

It wasn't until dinner that I realized that our little trip to the room on the tenth floor was about to lead Trina and me into a whole mess of trouble. Because that's when we realized that something had been stolen from that mysterious room.

And Trina and I were about to be blamed for it.

CHAPTER 3

That's Him!

The dining area at the Mountain Manor House was this gigantic round room at the opposite end of the hotel from the guest suites. It took us, like, ten minutes just to walk there. That's how long and rambling the hotel was. And when you walked into the dining room, you felt like you'd entered a really big school auditorium or something, all made out of wood and windows.

Wooden beams ran across the ceiling and met up at a point in the middle of the room, making the roof look like the cone of a party hat. The floor was constructed of polished wood, and if you weren't careful, you could go skidding across it and wipe out. The walls had windows that stretched from your knee to the ceiling, which meant that you could see the mountains and the clouds all around you. Tables with white linen cloths were set up around the room, and each table was named for a flower.

Our table that first night was Lilac 2. A candle with a small lamp shade completed the table setting, its light casting a homey glow and creating soft shadows.

Also on that first night I figured out what a course was. It's really just a different part of the meal that you eat at a different time. The first "course" was soup or an appetizer. I ordered the cheese and toast platter that night, while Carrie got the beef barley soup, which she complained about, of course. Mom and Dad ate froufrou seafood things: scallops wrapped in bacon and mini-crab cakes with a weird sauce.

The second course was a salad.

The third course was the main dish, and you could choose from six different things. I'm not too adventurous when it comes to food, so I just got the chicken.

And the fourth course was dessert. You can't pass that up, no matter what fancy name they give it.

So there we were, the Cantrell family, sitting in our spiffy outfits, bonding over dinner, eating our crème boules or whatever dessert we had ordered, when suddenly the old woman in the green jacket from the room on the tenth floor came barreling over to our table.

"That's him!" she croaked, pointing a trembling finger at me while balancing on her gnarly walking stick.

Behind her was a man who looked kind of important— an older guy, balding, and wearing a dark suit, white shirt, and tie.

Mom and Dad looked up from their desserts, shock clearly written all over their faces.

"Can we help you?" Dad said calmly, although I'm sure he was feeling far from calm. I know I wasn't feeling too calm at that moment, especially when I saw the twisted frown on the old woman's face. Her next words confirmed my apprehension.

"Your son stole something from the hotel!" the old woman accused, still pointing at me.

I wished I could have crawled into my chocolate tart and covered myself in fudge sauce, I was that embarrassed. Instead, all I could do was stare at her and her long, pointy finger, wiggling like a demented worm in my direction.

"Ben?" Mom said. I'm not sure if she was asking me to answer for myself, or if she was asking the old woman to clarify which son, even though Mom only has one. Either way, I figured that perhaps if I kept silent, the woman and her accusing worm finger would go away.

No such luck.

"I'm sure you're mistaken," my father said in my defense. "Our son has never stolen anything in his life."

"Tell that to the candlesticks!" said the woman with a thump of her stick.

"Candlesticks?" This was Mom, totally confused.

"Gretta, let me take over," said the important-looking guy. "Mr. and Mrs. Cantrell, correct?"

Mom and Dad nodded, still shock-faced.

"I'm Mr. Lowell, the hotel manager. Your son is believed to be in the possession of some very valuable candlesticks, which he obtained this afternoon while trespassing in a hotel room that is off limits to hotel guests."

It sounded like a bunch of gibberish to me, but Mom and Dad got the gist of it.

Carrie, on the other hand, did not.

"What? What's going on?" she screeched. "This is so embarrassing!" Made even more embarrassing by Carrie's screeching, I might add.

But Carrie was right, for once. That I was mortified was obvious—my face was as hot as a jalapeño pepper (and probably just as red), and I felt as if steam was coming off my ears. By this time, the entire dining room had grown quiet, with just ripples of voices whispering the question, "What's going on over there?" I could feel every eye in that swanky circular room boring into me, my family's included. The light and shadows cast by the candles had gone from warm and homey to eerie and threatening.

"Ben," Dad asked, "is there any truth to what Mr. Lowell is saying?"

"Yes and no," I answered honestly.

"See?" said the old lady, Gretta, triumphantly, an evil sparkle glinting from her eyes. It was then that I looked at her more closely. Although her clothes were the same, I noticed that her straw hat was missing, leaving her wiry hair to spring haphazardly around her weathered face like crumpled tinsel left over from Christmas.

"Ben," Dad said patiently, "what do you mean?"

"Well, I *was* in the room they're talking about. I even know the candlestick things. But I swear, Dad, I didn't take them."

Dad smiled, and Mom patted my hand. Carrie rolled her eyeballs, her favorite form of expression.

"You must have the wrong person," Dad said. "My son admits to being in the room, but not to taking anything."

"You can't take the word of a child," Gretta said, her eyes flashing at the mere thought of my word being better than hers.

Now, as I explained earlier, I don't know what, exactly, Dad does for work. I know that at the corporation he works for, he heads up important meetings all the time and that tons of people depend on him. But I've never seen the "work" Dad at home, only the "home" Dad, if that makes any sense. So I wasn't prepared to see the "work" Dad—the no-nonsense, professional Dad—make an appearance in the dining room that night. But suddenly, Pleasant Nice Dad was replaced by Cold Powerful Dad. I'm only thankful that his power wasn't directed at me. Mr. Lowell and Gretta, however, weren't so lucky.

"Mr. Lowell and Gretta, is it?" Dad asked, a hint of frostiness coating his words.

"Yes, sir," Mr. Lowell replied smartly.

Dad waited a beat before he continued, a second in which you could have heard an ant pick up a crumb and carry it across the dining room's polished floor on tiptoe.

"You have managed to ruin a perfectly good meal for my family. We paid good money to come to your hotel and enjoy a peaceful week. This is not a fortuitous beginning. If you have any concrete evidence that my son has your candlesticks, I will gladly review that evidence. However, my son claims his innocence, and I believe him. Furthermore, this entire matter could have been handled far more discreetly in the privacy of your office or our hotel room. Since you feel it is appropriate to handle such matters publicly, with the entire hotel staff and all the guests as witnesses, then let them bear witness to this: If you ever so falsely accuse my son again in such a public way, I will have every lawyer from here to Chicago on your doorstep, suing you for harassment."

Way to go, Dad!

Dad sat back in his chair, and with barely a blink, the powerful Darth Vader Dad disappeared and nice Dad was back again. "Do we understand each other?"

Mr. Hotel Manager didn't pull at his collar to get more air, but he looked like he wanted to. "I understand perfectly, Mr. Cantrell. I apologize for the disruption. Please excuse us."

Mr. Lowell bowed slightly, grabbed Grilling Gretta by the elbow, and the two left the dining room without another word. It took only a moment for the diners and waiters to snap to and begin buzzing—all about us, I'm sure.

"You were awesome, Dad!" I cheered, ready to high-five him across the table.

Dad was not in a high-fiving mood. "Ben, what were you doing trespassing?"

"I wasn't trespassing, Dad, honest! I was just exploring, and this one room wasn't locked, so I went inside. That Gretta lady came in and chased me and Trina out. I bet *she* took the candlesticks."

"Trina? Who's Trina?" Mom asked.

I shrugged like it was no big deal. "This girl I met."

For the first time all evening, Carrie perked up. "Girl? What girl? Oooo! Ben's got a girlfriend," she said all sing-songy.

"I do not!" (I felt like jalapeños again.)

Dad took a final sip of his coffee, threw his napkin on the table, and stood.

"Well, I think I've had enough drama for one day. We'll talk more about this when we get to our rooms."

We all stood up and followed Dad as he marched out of the dining room, trying to ignore everyone staring at us. It's a posh place, so no one actually pointed a finger or anything, but you could see people hiding behind their menus, giving us the once over.

Great! Instead of being just another faceless family, we'd become that family with the kid who's a thief. Wonderful.

I exited the dining room and trailed behind Mom and Dad and Carrie, like the sad caboose at the end of a slow train—until someone yanked my arm and derailed me.

CHAPTER 4

A Little History

You never know who (or what) might be grabbing you in a place that resembles a haunted castle. With Gretta's accusations echoing loudly in my brain, my first instinct was that she had snatched me from the safety of my parents and was going to clobber me with her stick if I didn't hand over the candlesticks. My next instinct was that some evil apparition had become likewise angry with me and had snared me with its ghoulish, misty arms. A bit over the top, I know, but the Mountain Manor House had that effect on me.

As I tried to make sense of where I was, I felt something smothering me, covering my whole body, and I struggled to free myself, flinging my arms wildly trying to fight off whatever had captured me. Rabid bats, perhaps? Yikes!

Then whoever—or whatever—had grabbed me spoke.

It was just Trina.

"I can't believe that happened!" she said from behind a bunch of coats in the closet she'd dragged me into.

I finally cleared the coats from my face and saw Trina's dark eyes staring back at me. "You saw that?"

"Who didn't? The entire dining room was staring at you."

"Great. Just what I need—to be the center of attention."

"I'm surprised that woman didn't accuse me, too," Trina said thoughtfully.

She had a point. Why hadn't her family been humiliated like mine?

I took a closer look at Trina and I have to admit, she looked really nice. Even though the light in the closet was dim, I could see that she was wearing a flowery, summer dress sort of thing and white sandals. Her hair was up in clips, not in a ponytail like it had been that afternoon. She looked almost grown-up.

"Maybe the old woman, Gretta, didn't recognize you," I said.

"Maybe," Trina wondered, chewing her lip. She shrugged her shoulders. "Well, there's only one thing to do now."

I was afraid of what Trina would say next, but of course I couldn't contain my curiosity.

"What's that?" I asked.

"We've got to clear our names."

"We've got to *what?*"

"Clear our names!" she said excitedly, her dark eyes shining.

"And how are we supposed to do that?"

"By finding those candlesticks, of course," she announced dramatically.

Trina was definitely asserting herself again, only this time it was on my behalf. I shook my head. "You're crazy. We'll never find those candlesticks. It would be like looking for a needle in a haystack."

Now it was Trina's turn to shake her head. "Why would anyone look for a needle in haystack? Have you ever heard of anyone actually doing that? Stupid expression."

"What does that have to do with anything?"

Just then, we heard someone call Trina's name out in the

hallway. "Shh! That's my dad. I've gotta go."

"Trina, I think we should just forget about this whole thing." I really did just want it to go away. I knew I hadn't taken those candle things, and my parents knew I hadn't, so what was the big deal?

Apparently, it was a big deal to Trina. She turned when she got to the closet door. "Meet me at nine o'clock tomorrow morning down by the boat rentals, okay?"

"I'm not sure—"

"Be there!" she insisted. Then she was gone.

I waited a few seconds, then I exited the closet after her. I walked slowly down the hallway to the big wooden staircase, trying to ignore the dark corners where the dim lighting didn't reach. You'd think I would have hurried through the old place to the safety of our rooms, but I was deep in thought. So instead, I slowly climbed the creaking steps to the second floor, then I continued down the musty hallway to our room. I knew there was no way I'd be able to meet Trina at nine o'clock the next day. I was certain my parents had stuff planned that would involve the entire family. The Cantrells were supposed to bond, after all.

However, at nine a.m., on the dot, I found myself in front of the boat rentals. Carrie had wanted to sleep in, and Mom and Dad had wanted to get up really early and tackle one of the hiking trails. I was kind of stuck in the middle, with no real desire to do either one. Instead, I found myself wandering down to meet Trina.

When I woke up that morning, I had decided that I wasn't going to meet her. In fact, I had convinced myself that our meeting in the coat closet the night before had been entirely a figment of my imagination. I had imagined Gretta and ghouls and bats snatching at me … hadn't I?

But when I stood on the metal balcony outside my room, as I listened to Carrie snore (she'd swear up and down that she didn't), and as I heard Mom and Dad leave their room, I gazed out at the scenery, which I hadn't seen yet. And I heard the lake and the boats calling to me.

It sounds dorky, I know, but the lake was really very beautiful. It was surrounded by trees and hiking trails, and the tall sides of the mountains rose all around it. The mountains and a stone tower, all the way at the top of the highest peak, were reflected upside down on the lake's glassy surface. I wondered if Mom and Dad were hiking up to that tower today, and I felt bad that I had decided not to go with them. No matter how I felt about the bonding thing, Mom and Dad had planned this vacation for all of us to be together. Not only had Carrie and I acted like babies about their vacation choice, but then I'd gone and gotten into trouble the first day. The first day!

I should've gone with them.

It was too late to fix things right then, so I meandered through the hotel. Next thing I knew, I was walking across the huge back porch, complete with dozens of rocking chairs, and then I found myself stepping down the few plank steps to the gravel walkway, eventually making my way over to the boat rentals. I glanced back at the hotel a few times, and once I thought I saw Gretta standing at one of the windows. When I blinked my eyes, all I could see was the sun bouncing off the panes. In the early-morning light, the hotel didn't look quite as creepy.

Trina was ready and waiting for me on the dock.

"Ben! Over here!" she shouted. If I had been at school

and some girl had hollered at me like that, I would have hidden inside the first handy locker. Instead, I waved and walked over. I was glad to know someone at this creepy place, and Trina wasn't all that bad, really. For a girl.

In fact, she looked sort of cute that morning, in her jean shorts and red-and-blue striped shirt—like she was going on a picnic or something. She smiled when she saw me and thrust a large book into my hands.

"What's this?" I asked.

"This will help us find the stolen candlesticks. I know it," she said confidently.

I began to flip through the pages. "What is it?"

"It's a book about the history of the hotel. I got it from the hotel library. I haven't looked through it yet, but I think if we find out what that room on the tenth floor was once used for, maybe we can find out why someone would want to steal the candlesticks."

"Couldn't they have been stolen just to sell? Because they're valuable or something?"

"Maybe, but I don't think so."

"Why not?"

"Well, if you were looking to steal something, would you walk up and down ten flights of stairs to do it?"

"Probably not," I agreed.

"Of course not. Also, if you were stealing stuff, wouldn't you steal more than just a couple of old candlesticks? Wouldn't you have taken, like, the pens from the desk? Or one of those old books? I bet they're worth a lot. So, I think someone stole those candlesticks for a specific reason."

Although I didn't agree with Trina at first, I thought she might have a point. But what reason would someone have to steal a couple of old candlesticks? "Maybe they were impor- tant to someone," I suggested.

"Exactly! Let's rent a paddleboat, and we can look at the book out on the lake."

So we rented a paddleboat and began pedaling away, the book propped up between us so it wouldn't get wet or fall in the water. We passed a few rowboats with fathers and sons fishing, and a few more paddleboats with teenage couples or grandparents with their grandchildren. Everyone waved at us as we passed by.

"Do you think they recognize me from last night at din- ner?" I asked Trina.

"I doubt it," Trina said. "One kid probably looks like another to them, you know?"

"I hope you're right. My sister, Carrie, is really worried that everyone will stare at her all week. She's sleeping in today, trying to avoid it."

"How old's your sister?" Trina asked.

"She's three years older than me—thirteen. She's going into the eighth grade, and that's all we hear about. She drives me nuts."

"At least you don't have a baby crying at all hours of the night who you have to watch sometimes when your mom needs to do laundry or something. I mean, I like Sarah, I really do, but sometimes I miss when it was just me and Mom and Dad. You know?"

I didn't really know, but I wondered if maybe that's how Carrie had felt after I came along. Hmm. Enlightening.

"Here, this looks like a good spot," Trina said as she stopped pedaling and hauled the book onto her lap. We'd maneuvered the boat into a small, secluded cove, surrounded on three sides by tall, thick pine trees. The other boats were colorful dots in the distance on the main part of the lake.

Now that we had some privacy, we began flipping through the book, looking for pictures of the room on the tenth floor or perhaps even a picture of the candlesticks themselves. As page after page after page flipped by, all the black-and-white old-fashioned photos began to blur together and look the same to me. Not to Trina, though. She found something new in each photograph, comparing the way the hotel looked then with how it looked now. It was kind of fun seeing the hotel through Trina's eyes. She didn't quite have the same impression of a haunted castle as I did.

Trina was just about to turn the page, when I saw a face in the book that looked familiar.

"Wait! Turn back!" I took the book from her and held it closely to my face, eyeing the picture closely, comparing it with the image in my mind.

Trina peered around the edge of the book to see which photograph had captured my attention. "That's not a room," she pointed out, disappointed at the object of my interest. "Those are just pictures of old people who used to live in the area or who stayed at the hotel."

"Yeah, but I know that picture," I said, pointing to one of the portraits. It was the portrait of a young man sitting at a desk, wearing glasses, and writing—writing with the same pens that had been on the desk in the room on the tenth floor.

The picture in the book of someone who had once stayed at the hotel was the same picture that was on the wall in the room on the tenth floor.

CHAPTER 5

The Saga Begins

"**A**re you sure?" Trina asked.

"I'm about ninety-five percent positive," I said with renewed energy. I *did* feel energized. For some reason, I felt like that picture was the key to solving who had stolen the candlesticks and the key to clearing my name.

I began pedaling the paddleboat furiously toward the dock. (Did you ever wonder why it's called a paddleboat? Shouldn't it be *pedal*boat?) "I can prove it, too," I told Trina. "I took a picture of the picture."

Trina's dark eyes widened. "Well, let's go!" And she began pedaling just as hard as I was.

I wanted to rush through the door to our hotel room, but then I remembered the snoring princess inside. Carrie the Cruel can be quite grouchy when her beauty sleep has been disrupted. I put a finger to my lips and cautioned Trina to be quiet. Then as silently as possible, I slipped the key into the lock and twisted. The doors and locks in the hotel were old-fashioned, meaning they made a big clicking sound when the lock turned.

Carrie, of course, heard it.

"You can come on in, Sneak. I'm awake," she called out.

I whispered to Trina to play it cool. I didn't want ol' Carrie getting any bright ideas that we had some bright ideas of our own. As nonchalantly as possible, I opened the door and strolled on in. "Hey, Sis. You finally got up."

Carrie was sitting in front of the desk. A mirror was propped up against the wall, and as she stabbed at her lids with a dark eyeliner pencil, she eyed me in the mirror, then saw I had company. With a smile like a cat who's just spotted a fat mouse, she turned around and licked her lips.

Really, actually licked them!

"Well, well. And who do we have here?" she purred. "Aren't you going to introduce me to your friend?"

"This is Trina," I said simply, with no explanation or further introduction. "We're going to take a walk around the hotel. I just want to get my camera." I thought I'd turn the tables on her. "Mom and Dad don't like when you wear make-up."

Carrie tossed her golden hair over her shoulder and blasted me with a sneer. "Mind your own business, Sneak." Then she crossed one leg over the other, showing that obnoxious attitude that I had so grown to love. I pretended not to notice. Turning her attention from me to Trina, she sneered a bit more.

"I'm Carrie," she said, sticking out a hand.

What thirteen-year-old does that? you're probably wondering. My nutso sister, that's who.

I had to give Trina credit. She took it all in stride, walked up to Carrie like she shook people's hands every day (maybe she did!), and shook. "Nice to meet you, Carrie. Ben's told me *all* about you."

Carrie wasn't stupid. She didn't miss the emphasis Trina had placed on the word *all.* Eyes narrowing, she said, "Really? What did the sneak say?"

"Just what a great sister you are," Trina said, making her eyes big so that she looked innocent and sincere.

Carrie continued to study her, not sure what to believe.

I grabbed my camera from my backpack. "Let's go," I said, dashing toward the door.

"Leaving so soon?" Carrie said.

"Places to go, people to see," Trina said, dropping Carrie's hand. "Maybe we'll see you down by the lake later."

"Yeah, maybe," Carrie said, becoming bored with me and Trina and turning back to the mirror to focus on her eyes again.

I heaved a huge breath when we finally closed the door.

"Your sister's weird!" Trina giggled. "I hope I'm not like that when I'm thirteen."

"Not many people are like Carrie. She's always had an attitude problem. But forget about her. Let's compare pictures."

Trina and I raced down the steps to the gigantic common room of the hotel. It was kind of like the hotel's lobby, only it had long wooden tables and chairs, where families could sit and talk, or on rainy afternoons play board games. There were leather couches next to three marble fireplaces. It also had several tall bookshelves, with signs that said, "Take a look, leave a book. Mountain Manor House's Guest Library."

Actually, to me it looked like one of those old, spooky libraries from a black-and-white horror movie. It wasn't exactly Frankenstein's laboratory, but the tables were long and dark, with lots of nicks and scratches—perfect for conducting experiments on. The bookcases were tall and overflowing with books—perfect for hiding secret passageways. And the corners were disturbingly dark—I could just picture spider webs the size of watermelons dangling up there, with juicy spiders just waiting for their next crunchy meal. The place

gave me the shivers, although Trina didn't seem to notice.

Trying to shake off the creeps, I joined Trina on one of the couches. "Is this where you got the book from?" I asked.

"Yup. I asked one of the hotel people if they had a book about the hotel's history. They showed me tons of stuff, but this one had the most pictures."

"Speaking of pictures." I turned on my digital camera, and Trina and I began scanning the images as they flashed by on the small screen. "Those must be the candlesticks," I said, pausing at one of the snapshots.

Trina peered closer. "Hmm. They're not very fancy or anything, are they?"

She was right. "Yeah, they're pretty plain. I guess that nixes the idea of someone stealing them to sell."

I flipped through a few more shots, and then there it was, the portrait.

"This is it," I said, holding the camera next to the page in the book that Trina held on her lap.

Trina studied the two, comparing them. "It *is* the same picture," she said slowly, excitement building. "Let's see who he is. 'Jerome Target,' it says."

Something began to niggle in the back of my brain, but I wasn't sure what it was. "Does it say anything else?"

"Yeah, listen to this: 'Jerome Target, well-known writer of books for children, including the *Saga of the*—'"

"*Stillwell Family*!" I finished for her.

"You know this guy?"

"I don't know him, but I know those books. Our reader at school had one of the Stillwell Saga stories in it."

"Really?" Trina looked impressed. "Do you remember what it was about?"

The niggling in my brain had started up again. "I'm trying to think," I said. "It was about this family, that owned a hotel…"

"Like, a hotel in the mountains maybe?" Trina prodded.

The niggling stopped then, as if to say, *Ta-da!* "It was! The family owned a hotel in the mountains. In the story we read, the Stillwell kids tried to solve the mystery of who had wounded a deer on hotel property. No one was supposed to hunt, if I'm remembering it right."

"Cool!" said Trina with a squeal. "I bet Jerome Target wrote about the Mountain Manor House."

"That *is* cool. But it still doesn't tell us who might have stolen the candlesticks."

"Let me take a look at the candlesticks photo again."

I handed the camera over to Trina and showed her how it worked. She focused in on the photo, then suddenly froze, as if something was wrong.

"What is it?" I asked, peering at the picture myself.

"Look at the doors in the background."

I took the camera from her and looked closely.

"Do you see it?" Trina whispered.

I studied the picture harder, and then I did, indeed, see *it*. On one of the lacy white curtains, I could just make out what looked like a shadow, formed by a figure inside the room. However, inspecting the photo more closely, I realized that the shadow was actually cast by something that was *outside* on the balcony. And looking even closer, I could see that the floor-to-ceiling window/door was open, just slightly.

And the shadow looked like a person—a person wearing a baseball cap.

CHAPTER 6

Oh, Henry!

"**S**omeone else was inside the room!" Trina whispered loudly.

I was just as shocked as she was—and a little creeped out, too. While I had been in there, snapping away with my camera, someone had been standing right outside those balcony doors, watching me.

Then something else occurred to me. "That's probably why the door to the room was unlocked in the first place—someone had already opened it to go inside."

"And when you went strolling in, you scared whoever it was, and he or she ran out onto the balcony."

"Only whoever it was didn't expect me to start taking pictures—"

"—and for his or her shadow to show up on your camera," Trina finished for me.

"So whoever was on the balcony—" I continued.

"—probably stole the candlesticks!" Trina finished again.

Whoa! Mental breakthrough!

Trina and I slumped back on the couch, exhausted, as if we had just hiked up and down all the trails at the Mountain Manor House.

"So, how do we figure out who our mystery person is?" I wondered out loud.

"Maybe whoever it was left behind a clue," Trina said, sitting up again. "Let's see if the room is locked."

I didn't have a better idea, so with camera in hand (me) and book in arms (Trina), we raced up ten flights of wooden steps, creaks and all, till we reached the top. Then we tore down the hallway to the room on the end.

Just like yesterday, the door was closed with the "Do Not Enter" sign displayed prominently at eye level. I turned the glass doorknob, just like yesterday, but unlike yesterday, the door didn't budge.

"Locked," I said, stating the obvious.

"Drat," Trina said, disappointed. "I guess that was pushing our luck."

"How about we look *outside* the room," I suggested.

"We *are* outside the room."

"No, I mean *outside* outside."

"Like, outdoors?"

"Sure. Maybe whoever was standing on the balcony dropped something over the railing."

"Good idea," Trina agreed.

We dashed back down the hall and down the stairs, but slowed up when we came to the big common room. Trying to walk as innocently as possible, we sauntered through, put the hotel-history book back on the shelf, then roamed casually over to the door leading outside. Flinging open the door, we dashed across the porch and down the steps.

It took us a while to figure out which balcony most likely belonged to the room on the tenth floor. It didn't seem like it should be so difficult, but the hotel wasn't built evenly. There were rounded rooms and towers and spires, and some parts of the roof had peaks and other parts had valleys.

Every room had a balcony. We kept the lake on our left side, with the hotel on our right, and we just kept walking and walking until the hotel came to an end—or at least the very highest part of the roof did. And we were so busy looking up and pointing and counting balconies and floors and concentrating on which might belong to the room on the tenth floor, that we didn't notice when someone else was on the path until we nearly bumped into him.

That someone else was a man holding a rake.

And wearing a baseball cap.

I froze when I saw him, thinking, *Could this be our candlestick snatcher? Could this be the person who was in the room the same time we were?*

Trina, of course, was not frozen up like me. She found her courage very quickly.

"Excuse us!" she said brightly. "We weren't watching where we were going."

"I'll say," said the man. He seemed a bit grumpy, but not really angry with us. "You must be looking for the Huckleberry Hiking Trail."

"Huckle—? Oh! Yeah, we are," I said before Trina could correct him. I wasn't sure if she would correct him, but I didn't want to take any chances. I'd known Trina for less than a day, but what I already knew for sure was that she liked to speak her mind—and speak it often. I thought the less said here, the better.

"Well, just keep going, and you'll find the trail a few yards up that way," the man with the baseball cap said, pointing up the path in a vague direction.

"It must be so cool to work here," Trina blurted out. See what I mean? I would have happily ventured up the path to

keep up the premise that we were hikers, but no, not Trina. She had to dive headfirst into an interrogation. From cop shows I'd seen on TV, I knew that the baseball cap connection was really just circumstantial evidence and didn't prove a thing. Yet that detail didn't stop Trina from doing some digging.

The man pushed up his cap, giving us a better view of his face. I guessed that he was about the same age as my parents, maybe a bit older. His face was tan and a little crinkly, and his hair appeared to be red under the ball cap, but not bright red—almost like it was graying slightly. He wore dark green pants and a tan T-shirt, and his hands were covered with gardening gloves.

He smiled slightly at Trina. "It can be fun to work here, sure," he said.

"I bet you must know the names of all the plants and stuff, too, since you're outside with them," Trina went on.

What was with the twenty questions? Trina seemed to have something in mind, so I let her ask away, even though my instincts kept nudging me in the stomach, telling me to take that hike up Huckleberry Trail.

"I know a fair number of them, I reckon," said the man.

"Wow! Maybe you can tell us sometime, when you're not working. What's your name?"

A-ha!

"I don't usually give tours," he said, beginning to rake the grass alongside the hotel—right below the balconies that lined up with the room on the tenth floor.

"But if you *did*," Trina insisted, "who would we ask for?"

"I'm Henry," he said, after a few more rakes. "Henry Gershin."

"Well, thank you, Mr. Gershin," Trina said. "Maybe

we'll see you around."

And with that, she hurried off, with me trailing after her.

As soon as we were out of earshot of Henry, we ducked down another path—one that led back to the hotel.

"So, what do you think of Mr. Henry Gershin?" Trina asked.

"I think he acted kinda suspicious," I said. "I swear, when we first bumped into him, with the light shining behind him, he looked like he could have been the guy on the balcony in the baseball cap."

"I know! How freaky was that? *And,* he was raking the grass below the balconies. That's suspicious, too."

"Yeah, like he was looking for something, only he was pretending to work."

Trina and I continued down the trail, coming up on the other side of the hotel. We both were silent, thinking about Henry and the candlesticks and wondering how the two might be connected.

"I've got an idea," I said. "I don't know why we didn't think of this before." Probably because it was a scary idea that involved confronting an important member of the hotel staff. But I had a few questions about the missing candlesticks. Like, who noticed that they were missing in the first place? And how did Grouchy Gretta find out? After all, I knew the candlesticks were there when we left, so Gretta must have known it, too. Why would she accuse me? I posed my questions to Trina, and she agreed that they were good ones and that we needed to find the answers.

"But how?" she asked.

And that was the one question I *didn't* want to answer because I didn't like the solution. "Mr. Lowell," I replied.

"Who's that?"

"That's the manager guy who talked to us last night at dinner—the guy with Gretta. I wanted to avoid him, but I can't think of any other way to find out about this stuff."

"Hmm. The manager," Trina considered. She shrugged. "Why not? Let's give it a shot."

We went back into the hotel and found the manager's office down a hallway marked "Employees Only." Mr. Lowell's name was on the door, but the door was closed, so we knocked. We waited for him to say, "Come in," and when he did, we were in for quite a surprise.

For lined up all around Mr. Lowell's office were dozens and dozens of … you guessed it.

Candlesticks.

CHAPTER 7

Lowell and Behold

"**M**r. Lowell?" I asked politely.

Mr. Lowell was perched behind a big desk, facing the door. He was reading some papers in a folder, his eyebrows drawn together, giving his face a sinister look. At dinner the night before, he'd looked rather sheepish and silly, especially when Dad had laid into him. Now he looked more like the man of power that he was, and I didn't have my dad to run interference for me. It was just me, Trina, and Mr. Lowell with the sinister eyebrows and the receding hairline.

He raised his head when we entered, and his eyebrows arched slightly with mild interest.

"Can I help you children?" he asked, just as mildly.

I cleared my throat. It was hard for me to admit to him that I was the one he'd accused of stealing the candlesticks, especially since I hadn't done it, but it seemed like the quickest way to start. "Um, sir, I'm the kid from last night? At dinner? The one you asked about the candlesticks?" (Why was I saying it like they were questions? No question about it: I was the accused here.)

Mr. Lowell's eyes sharpened slightly and he closed the folder on his desk. "Why, it is you," he said. "Have you come here to confess, then?"

"Confess?" Trina jumped in before I could even

process the fact that he still thought I was the thief. "Ben has nothing to confess. He didn't do it!"

"I see," said Mr. Lowell, sitting back in his chair but leaving his hands on the folder, his brows once again angling strangely over his eyes. Give him a spindly mustache and he could have been the typical villain in an old Western. "Then why are you here?"

"Well, sir," I began, fidgeting, "we'd like to find the candlesticks for you."

"That isn't necessary," he said with a flick of his wrist. "I'm sure they will turn up somewhere."

"You didn't seem to think so last night," I reminded him. "Besides, it looks like candlesticks are pretty important to the hotel. You've sure got enough of them in here."

Mr. Lowell looked around his office, and his face began to beam, those ol' eyebrows dancing on his forehead. "This is my private collection," he said proudly. "I've been collecting antique candlesticks for years."

"Do you have any that match the ones that were stolen?" Trina questioned.

"Why do you ask?" Mr. Lowell said, his eyes getting sharp and squinty again, the brows diving dangerously low.

"Well, it would help us find the stolen ones if we knew what they looked like," I said.

Mr. Lowell seemed to consider that for a moment, then shook his head. "I don't believe there are any candlesticks in my collection that resemble the ones in that room."

The next question I needed to ask was obvious. "Um … well … what was that room used for, anyway?"

"It was actually the private room of a writer named Jerome Target. He wrote the *Saga of the—*"

"—*Stillwell Family* books," I finished for him. "Yeah, we know. He used to write in that room?"

"That's right. He liked to write during the day, when most of the guests were outdoors and the hotel was quiet. Only the main rooms of the hotel had electricity at that time, so the guests used candles. Mr. Target liked to write by natural daylight."

"Cool," I said. I really *did* think it was cool. I had read a Jerome Target story in school and now I had seen where he had written it. Excellent!

"Mr. Lowell," Trina said, getting us back on track, "who accused Ben of stealing the candlesticks?"

"That was Gretta," Mr. Lowell answered. "In fact, she was quite distraught about the whole thing. Said that a maid had told her about the missing candlesticks. Then Gretta told me how you had been in Mr. Target's room."

"I was only in the room in the first place because it was unlocked," I told Mr. Lowell.

"Unlocked?" His squinty eyes looked sincerely perplexed. "How odd. We always keep Mr. Target's room secure."

"Why?" I asked. "I mean, I would think guests would want to see the room where a famous author worked. It would be like a … a … museum, sorta."

"That's a good point, Ben." Mr. Lowell seemed to be warming up to me. "I would like nothing better than to acknowledge Jerome Target's connection with the hotel. But when Mr. Target died, he specified in his will that he wanted his room to remain closed to the public. I don't know why, but those were his wishes. And we try to abide by them to this day."

"But that's so strange," Trina said, echoing the same thought that was going through my head.

Mr. Lowell shrugged. "Be that as it may, Mr. Target's room has always been closed to outside eyes. You should feel very lucky, actually, that you had a chance to see it."

"Yeah, so lucky that someone accused Ben of stealing," Trina muttered under her breath.

"Who was the maid who told Gretta about the candlesticks?" I asked, not wanting Trina's negativity to get Mr. Lowell angry. He seemed fairly accommodating so far, answering our questions and providing information about Jerome Target and his writing room. The last thing we needed was to alienate him.

Mr. Lowell folded his hands on his desk and thought a bit. "I think it was Patrice. Yes, I believe Gretta mentioned Patrice's name."

"Could we talk to her?"

Mr. Lowell smiled down at us—even though he was sitting at his desk—like he had a secret he was hiding. His eyebrows were now level on his forehead. "And what do you hope to learn by doing that?"

"Like, when she noticed that the candlesticks were missing. And maybe who else could have been in the room. Maybe she can help prove that I didn't take them."

Mr. Lowell's smile became even more secretive—almost like he was holding back a laugh. "I don't see how it can hurt. I'm not sure where in the hotel she might be, but I'll have Neez take you to her."

"Knees?" Trina and I said together.

"Short for Ebenezer," Mr. Lowell said. "He's been at the hotel for years. Sort of a handyman around here. Knows the building and the staff like the back of his hand. He's just down the hall. Neez!" Mr. Lowell shouted.

And sure enough, in walked an old man about the same age as Gretta. He wasn't stooped over or anything. In fact, he seemed quite sprightly for an old guy.

"Yes, Mr. Lowell?" His voice sounded strong, not rough or sandpapery like you might expect.

"Could you help these children find Patrice? They have some questions for her."

"Certainly, Mr. Lowell. She's probably just finished cleaning up the massage rooms."

Massage rooms?

So we thanked Mr. Lowell and followed Neez back into the hallway, past the common room, and down another hallway. I felt like we were in a maze, with one corridor leading into another, which then sprouted yet another endless passageway through the hotel—a dimly lit tunnel of faded flowered carpeting and old paneled doors that led to who knows where.

Trina and I were whispering to each other when Neez suddenly turned around and said, "What do you need Patrice for? Did you lock yourselves out of your rooms?"

Trina and I cracked up at that.

"No!" I gasped, trying not to laugh too hard. "Patrice is the one who noticed that the candlesticks in Jerome Target's writing room were missing."

"And Ben here's the one who was accused of taking them," Trina joined in.

Did I mention that Trina likes to assert herself?

I shot Trina a look, wishing she wouldn't keep telling people that.

Neez slowed down and waited for us to catch up to him.

"You don't say? You don't look like a criminal to me."

"I'm not. That's why we want to talk to Patrice. We thought maybe she could tell us when she noticed the candlesticks were missing and what happened next."

Neez began to rub his chin with one hand, propping that arm up at the elbow with his other hand. "Hmm … I can see your dilemma. I always told Lowell that no good would come of that room being closed off."

"You mean Mr. Target's room?" I asked.

"Sure. That room should either be open to the public, or the items removed. As it is, so much mystery surrounds Jerome Target that his things have become very valuable. I'm surprised the candlesticks didn't go missing a lot sooner."

"What do you mean, 'mystery?'" Trina asked.

"You don't know?"

Trina and I looked at each other, then back at Neez and shook our heads.

"Why, when Jerome Target died, they never found his body."

A Family Affair

Gulp. "His body?" I repeated.

"Yes," Neez continued casually, as if he hadn't just dropped a huge bomb. "Jerome Target went out for a hike one afternoon, like he always did … only he never returned."

"And people think he died?" Trina asked.

"Jerome Target had a favorite coat and an old hat he always wore on his hikes, and he also never went out without his walking stick. When he didn't return by dinnertime, the hotel sent out a search party."

Neez turned down one dark and dingy hallway, then another. I was vaguely aware that Trina and I would never be able to find our way back, but I was too caught up in Neez's story to ask for directions. "So what happened?"

Neez paused in front of a door. "Well, it was pretty late when the search party began looking. They couldn't search for very long because it got dark, but they started early again the next morning."

"And?" Trina said.

"They followed the trail that Jerome liked to hike, but about halfway along they saw something truly horrible."

I gulped. I seemed to be doing a lot of that. "What?"

"They found Jerome's jacket and hat torn to pieces, shredded, and his walking stick covered with blood."

Trina and I gasped.

"What do you think happened?" I whispered.

"Folks around here believe that Jerome was attacked by a bear or mountain lion."

"A lion?" Trina whispered back.

"Back then, mountain lions were pretty common around here," Neez clarified. "But not now—you don't have to worry," he added, taking in our startled faces.

Pushing open the door in front of us, he ushered us inside. "Now, let's see if Patrice is about."

Trina and I were still too stunned to process what we had just heard. No body? Attacked by bears? Eaten by lions? It was like something you'd read in a book, not hear about in real life. It was totally creepy.

We were trying to let the news about poor Jerome Target settle in, imagining what it would be like to be dragged off by a wild animal with no one around to help, when suddenly Neez and a woman stood before us.

"Patrice," Neez began, "these children have a few questions for you."

Trina and I looked up … and up … and up. Standing next to Neez was the tallest woman I'd ever seen.

"Yes?" she said haughtily, like she was the queen of clean, or something. "What is it? I'm very busy."

I found my tongue first. "Miss Patrice," I began. "Um … we were wondering, well, when did you first see that the candlesticks in the room on the tenth floor were missing?"

Patrice pursed her lips together really tight, like she had just sucked on the sourest lemon drop on the planet. She wore a really ugly hotel uniform of brown pants and a maroon-and-beige striped shirt. A feather duster dangled

from one hand while a rag hung from the other. My eyes became riveted to the feathers of the duster when I noticed that they were trembling, and when I looked up at Patrice's face, I saw that it was turning red. Beet red.

"Did Gretta put you up to this?" she barked at us.

"What? No!" I insisted. "Gretta said something about the candlesticks, but Mr. Lowell told us about you."

"Humph!" she said, rattling the rag and duster in the air. "I wouldn't be surprised if that old woman spread some more lies around the hotel about me."

"What lies?" Trina asked.

"She accused me of stealing those stupid candlesticks, that's what!"

It took a moment for Trina and I to pick our jaws up off the floor. When gravity finally released the hold on my mouth, I said, "But that doesn't make any sense. She blamed *me* for taking them."

Neez decided to chime in at this point. "Patrice, why don't you start from the beginning?"

Patrice waved her cleaning tools in the air. "As you know, Neez, Jerome Target's room only gets dusted about once a month. Well, it was time, and it was my turn to do it. I went up to the tenth floor and was surprised to find the room already opened. When I went inside, I saw Gretta standing next to the desk, looking down at it."

"What was she doing?" Trina asked.

"Nothing much that I could see, just looking at it closely. I saw her reach out and brush her hand lightly over that old pen set on the desk. I knew it was pretty dusty because no one had cleaned it in a month, so I spoke up."

I was curious. "What did you say?"

"I warned Gretta that it would be dirty, but I guess I startled her. She turned around and started yelling at me."

Yelling? I thought to myself. Out loud, I said, "What did she say?"

"She started rambling on about how no one was supposed to be in the room and what was I doing there. When I told her that it was time for the room's cleaning, she looked around quickly, then started yelling about the missing candlesticks. And accusing me of taking them."

"Which, of course, you hadn't," Trina interjected.

"Of course not!" Patrice bristled. "I take my job and responsibilities at Mountain Manor House very seriously. Which is why I should probably get back to work now."

She turned around to leave, but I stopped her with one more question. "What did you say to Gretta when she accused you of stealing?"

Patrice looked guilty. "Something I probably shouldn't have said, but I was so angry, I couldn't help myself."

"What?" Trina and I asked in unison.

"I said that maybe *she* was the one who had stolen them. After all, she was in the room before I was, and I hadn't seen any candlesticks since I'd entered."

Neez chuckled. "I bet Gretta didn't like that."

"Not one bit. Next thing I knew, she was storming down the stairs, mumbling under her breath. I went after her, knowing where she was headed, and sure enough, she marched right into Mr. Lowell's office and claimed that I'd stolen the darn things. When I told Mr. Lowell I had just entered the room for the first time that day, Mr. Lowell asked Gretta if anyone else had been in the room."

My stomach dropped to my feet. I knew what Gretta must have said next. "She named me, didn't she?"

"You?"

"I'm Ben, Ben Cantrell."

Patrice looked at me like I had three heads. It was obvious that she didn't recognize my name. Then another thought occurred to me. "What time did all this happen?"

"It was toward the end of the day," Patrice confirmed. "The Target room was my last stop of the day."

"Was it dinnertime?" I felt I had to know *exactly.*

"Yes, it was. The hotel was quiet, which meant that most of the guests were at the opposite end, in the dining room."

Trina looked at me meaningfully, then back to Patrice. "What did Gretta do next?"

"Well, it was really quite strange. She grabbed Mr. Lowell by his sleeve and dragged him out of the office. But I have no idea where they went."

"Well, I do," I said, feeling miserable. I suspected that this was when Gretta had brought Mr. Lowell to the dining room to point her wobbly finger at me.

I was so busy feeling sorry for myself that I almost missed Trina's next question. "Well, if *we* didn't take them and *you* didn't take them, then who do you think *did* take them, Patrice?"

Patrice shrugged her shoulders. "I have no idea and I'm not really interested. It's not my problem."

"But if you *were* interested…" Trina persisted.

Patrice shrugged again, letting loose a stream of dust from the feathers. "I wouldn't put it past Gretta herself to take them. Or maybe even that strange son of hers."

Our mouths hit the carpet again. "Son? What son?"

"Why, Henry Gershin, of course."

CHAPTER 9

Maybe I Took Them

"**H**enry Gershin is Gretta's son?"

"Yes," Patrice assured us. "Now if that's all, I need to get back to work."

As I watched Patrice walk to the door, I finally noticed our surroundings—flowerpots with colorful blooms and cabinets full of lotions. A small waterfall tinkled on a windowsill, a ceiling fan droned lazily overhead, and the walls were painted a soothing pale blue. The carpeting was cream colored and very soft looking. In fact, the whole room was really modern.

"What *is* this place?" I asked Neez as he led us out the door and back onto the old worn carpeting we were used to seeing.

"These are the massage rooms."

"They're very swanky," I commented.

"The hotel updated them about a year ago."

"Oh." I was still in too much shock about the Gretta-Henry connection to say much else.

Not Trina. "Is Gretta really Henry's mom?"

"Yep," Neez said as, thankfully, he led us back through the hallways. Without a map or a compass, I don't think Trina and I ever would have found our way back to the lobby through the labyrinth of halls.

Then Trina started to giggle. "So Gretta's name is really (snicker, snicker) Gretta Gershin?"

I started snickering with her. "Gretta Gershin!"

Neez got really serious for a moment. "Well, Gershin's her married name, you know."

"Do you know what her name was before she got married?" I don't know why I asked. Just curious again, I guess.

"Nope," Neez replied shortly. "Now, if you kids will excuse me, I have some of my own business to attend to." And with that, Neez was gone, disappearing down another dark hallway, away from the main part of the hotel.

Trina and I continued on our way when suddenly the giant clock in the common room began to chime. We hadn't heard it all day, but now it made its presence known, as if shaking us back to reality.

"Oh, no," I moaned. "Is it really one o'clock? I'm sure I'm late for lunch or something."

"Me, too," Trina said. "I should probably check in with my family. Let's try to meet up later, okay?"

"Okay, I'll look for you."

"I think we made a lot of progress, though," she said.

"Really? How?"

"Well, now we've got a ton of suspects."

I scratched my head. "We do?"

"Sure. Think about it. Obviously, we've got Gretta. And maybe even Henry."

I was starting to warm up to the idea of suspects. "And what about Mr. Lowell with all those candlesticks?"

"Right!" Trina beamed. "We'll have this mystery solved in no time, and your name will be free and clear."

After we said goodbye, I met up with my family in our

rooms. They were just heading down to lunch, so I went with them. I saw Trina and her family in the dining room, but our tables weren't near each other, so we just waved and smiled. Carrie made some stupid comment about my new friend, but I (basically) ignored her. I was busy sifting through all the new information we had about who might have stolen the candlesticks.

And about Jerome Target. I was beginning to think that he might be the key to figuring out where the candlesticks were, but I couldn't explain why. I just couldn't focus on any one of the gazillion ideas jumping through my head long enough to figure it out.

It seemed unlikely that Jerome Target could be at the center of our mystery because he'd been dead for, like, fifty years. The hotel was certainly old enough to have ghosts lingering around, but the idea of Jerome Target thumping around on his walking stick and stealing candlesticks was just too creepy to believe. So instead of thinking of Jerome Target's ghost, I began thinking of Jerome Target the writer. It was then that I realized I really didn't know much about Jerome Target at all.

Except that he was maybe killed by a bear or a lion.

And that they never found his body.

I was back to Jerome's ghost again. Great.

My parents thought it would be nice if the whole family hung out at the beach after lunch. It wasn't a real beach, but a lake beach. I had seen it from the paddleboat that Trina and I had rented. It wasn't very big, but it did have sand and it looked like fun. And maybe some fresh mountain air would clear my head of ghosts. So I agreed to go. I figured that Trina probably had things to do with her family, too, and anyway, it would give me time to really think about Jerome Target and our list of suspects.

After lunch, we returned to our rooms to change into bathing suits and grab beach stuff. Carrie took forever picking the right suit, so I told my parents I'd meet everyone downstairs in the common room.

I was leaning against one of the marble fireplaces, gazing around at the dark paneled room and thinking of Jerome Target, when I focused on the hotel's lending library. Now, I had read one of Jerome Target's stories in class, but I couldn't remember the details very well, so I pushed off from the fireplace and asked an employee if the library had any of the Stillwell Family stories. Sure enough, there was a whole bookcase full. I was just pulling one from the shelf when my family entered the room. We headed outside.

We walked along the hotel, close to where Trina and I had run into Henry Gershin. I even glanced up at what I thought might be Jerome Target's room, but I didn't see anything suspicious, nor did I see Henry. Carrie was whining that the walk to the beach was too long, and my parents were chattering away about the things they had seen on their hike, and I was trying to tune them all out and focus on what Trina and I had learned that day.

We arrived at the beach, ready to do some Cantrell family bonding. We spread out our towels, and Mom and Dad dragged me into the water with them. Carrie would have none of it, but I did see her look around with interest at a group of teenage guys doing cannonballs off the wooden pier.

Finally, Mom and Dad released me from lake duty, and I swam back to shore while they continued to float around in a big inner tube. I swear, you'd think Mom and Dad were the kids on this trip. They were having such a good time, all easygoing smiles and lighthearted conversations.

I plunked down next to Carrie who was lying on her stomach, sunbathing. She wasn't snoring yet, but I expected to hear that lovely chainsaw melody coming from her in no time. I was even halfway thinking of causing some sort of commotion so the teenage boys would wander over to investigate and hear the snoring princess for themselves.

But then I remembered the book I'd brought and the next thing I knew, I was caught up in Jerome Target's tales of the Stillwell family and their adventures at a mountain manor house. I could picture the scavenger hunts in the walled garden (although I hadn't visited the garden yet) and the picnics at the lookouts along the hiking trails (although I hadn't been to a lookout yet, either). Each story ended with a march up to the tower house at the top of the highest peak, a party, and singing and fireworks.

Okay, so the stories were a little corny. They were written in the 1940s after all, so they weren't exactly modern. The family didn't do anything high-tech, like take trips to Europe or visit amusement parks and ride monster roller coasters. But something about the stories made me feel really nice inside. The family was so close, and they really cared about each other. In fact, the family was a little like my family and Trina's family combined. There was an older sister, a middle son, a baby sister, and a mom and dad. They always got along and helped each other when problems came up.

Not like me and Carrie the Cruel.

I was reading the fourth story, about the family's adventure trying to save a wounded baby bear, when I remembered how Jerome Target might have died. Pretty creepy.

Then I came across something that was even creepier. The animal doctor in the story who helped the Stillwell family was named Dr. Varner.

Dr. Ebenezer Varner. Ebenezer. As in Neez.

Now, I didn't know Neez's last name, but I thought it was a pretty big coincidence that the name Ebenezer, which I'd barely heard before, had come up twice in the same day. Sure, it was just more circumstantial evidence like Henry's cap, but it was still suspicious, and I figured that it gave Trina and me another angle to work with.

I was just about to mark my place in the book when Carrie sat up as if someone had nudged her from her sleep.

Unfortunately, it seemed as if she'd gotten up on the wrong side of the blanket.

"This place is so lame," she said. "There's nothing to do here. And would you look at Mom and Dad? Has anyone told them lately that they're, like, *old?*"

I glanced at Mom and Dad, wrestling on the inner tube. "They're having fun," I countered, wanting to add, *unlike you.* "Besides, I think this place is okay."

"Oh, really?" Carried shifted her legs toward me. "Could that be because of your new friend?"

"Cut it out, Carrie."

"Ooo-oo! A little sensitive, are we?"

"You'd be sensitive too if someone falsely accused you of stealing," I snapped at her.

Then Carrie said the strangest thing. She drew up her legs and wrapped her arms around her knees, cocked her head, and gave me a sideways smile. "Who knows?" she suggested mysteriously. "Maybe *I* took them."

CHAPTER 10

A Picture Is Worth a Thousand Words

"**W**hat are you talking about?" I must have heard her wrong, right? Nope.

"Well," said Carrie, fluffing her hair. "Everyone made such a big deal about those stupid things that were stolen."

Stupid things?

"I don't know why they blamed you," she went on. "I mean, I'm in this family, too. How do they know that I didn't take them?"

Carrie is such a spaz sometimes. "You *want* to be blamed for something you didn't do?"

"Did you see the way everyone was staring at us?"

"I thought that embarrassed you!"

"Oh, it did. But then I thought that maybe it could work to my advantage."

I could only shake my head and wonder at the way Carrie's mind worked. "What are you talking about?"

"Well, the next time something like that happens, I'm going to be prepared."

The next time? I had just reached two conclusions: One, Carrie *didn't* take the candlesticks. And two, she was thinking of doing something stupid to get attention.

"Carrie, I don't know what you mean by 'the next time,' but I hope you're not planning to do anything crazy."

"You mean like you stealing from the hotel?"

"I didn't steal anything!" I was steamed. It was one thing for people at the hotel to believe I was a thief. After all, they didn't know me. But it was another thing for my sister to believe it. We were family, for crying out loud. Wasn't family supposed to stick up for each other?

Apparently not.

"Look," Carrie said seriously, slapping her legs back down against the blanket and turning to face me. "I'm a teenager now. I can't be bothered with playing baby games, like camping and canoeing. Or floating in an inner tube like Mom and Dad. But if I can find a boyfriend, this trip won't be such a complete waste, you know?"

I didn't know, but I wasn't about to tell her that. Instead, I asked, "How are you going to get around the parents?"

Carrie swung her arm down the beach, where Mom and Dad were busy hauling the inner tube out of the lake. "They are too busy *bonding* to even notice what I'm up to."

With that, Carrie stood up, brushed invisible grains of sand off her bathing suit, and sashayed her way over to the dock full of guys. I couldn't hear what she said to them, but I did hear the guys laugh. Then Carrie strutted back to the blanket, a big smile plastered on her very smug face.

"Now *that* was fun!" she declared, plopping down beside me on the blanket once again.

I didn't know what she had said, and to be honest, I really didn't care. If Carrie thought the Mountain Manor House was lame, I thought her attempts at getting the guys' attention were lame too, and totally uninteresting. So I went back to reading my book and although I crossed Carrie's name off my suspect list, I kept her in my mind all the same. She might not want anything to do with her little brother or this lame family vacation, but I was still worried about her.

I didn't get a chance to talk to Trina for the rest of the day. She was busy doing her family stuff and I was busy doing mine. However, she did pass a note to me at dinner, and the next day after breakfast we met by the paddleboats again. We sat on the edge of the dock and swung our legs back and forth over the side.

I showed Trina the page in the book about Dr. Ebenezer Varner while the boats glided across the lake and the white cottony clouds slid across the blue sky.

"What do you think?"

"I think we should add Neez to our list of suspects," she replied, once again echoing my own ideas.

I gave it a moment or two more of thought—although I'd spent the whole previous evening thinking about it— then shook my head. Something seemed out of sync to me. "It doesn't make any sense, though. Neez didn't seem guilty at all yesterday when we questioned Patrice. He seemed really helpful."

"True. Still, I think he might have something to do with all this."

Something started to niggle at my brain again. I began to think out loud. "Let's list what we know for a fact, okay? Fact One: We know that the room where the candlesticks were was once used by Jerome Target. Fact Two: We know that Jerome Target wrote children's stories based here at the hotel."

"And don't forget Fact Three."

I shivered. "How could I? Fact Three: Jerome Target died and his body was never found." The niggling in my head got stronger. "Hmm. Is it possible... ? No, that's crazy."

"What? What's crazy?"

"Well..." I felt silly even thinking it, much less voicing it out loud. The idea was ludicrous, preposterous. "Could it be that Jerome Target didn't really die?"

"But they found his stuff, and he never showed up again," Trina said reasonably.

"I know, but they never found his body. Could it be that he just disappeared and went off somewhere to live his life someplace else, like for privacy or something?"

"But where would he have gone? And don't you think someone would have figured it out?"

"Yeah, I guess." I paused for a moment. "But what if he came back years later to, like, work at the hotel—as a handyman or something?"

"You mean like Neez?"

"Exactly!"

Trina stopped swinging her legs and just stared at me. "You think Neez could be Jerome Target?"

"It's possible, I guess. What do you think?"

"I don't know. It seems a little out there."

"Yeah, I know. Out there." I felt deflated. I was so sure that Trina would back me up that her doubt was disappointing. But she was probably right—the notion of Neez being Jerome Target *did* seem far-fetched. My insane idea was too outlandish even for Trina.

We stared at the lake for a few moments, watching the paddleboats and rowboats, each wrapped up in our own thoughts of Neez, Jerome, and a long-lost body.

Finally Trina spoke, breaking the silence that had wrapped around us as we muddled through our own ideas.

"It does make a little bit of sense, I guess. I'm trying to think if Neez looks anything like Jerome Target. Or the picture we've seen of Jerome Target, at least."

"I think we have to get that big book about the hotel again and compare. If Neez *is* Jerome, maybe we can find a picture of him after Jerome died. The picture would have to look like both Neez and Jerome Target. That way, we could tie them both together."

"Don't you think someone would have recognized him?"

I hated to admit it, but Trina had a point. Still… "Not if no one who knew him was still here when he came back." Okay, it was a stretch, but it was all we had to go on.

We swung our legs back onto the dock and went into the hotel. The big hotel-history book was right where we'd left it. I grabbed the book from the shelf, and we sat down and began looking through it again. This time, we started from the end of the book and worked our way backward, looking for a picture of a man named Ebenezer. We came up with nothing… the big goose egg.

We kept looking anyway, searching the faces and scanning the names. It was a little spooky, gazing into all those smiling eyes of young people who would now be either very old or very dead. They were so full of life and happiness back then, wearing old-fashioned clothes and silly grins, looking like they owned the world.

We were peering at just such a picture, of a group of young people in their twenties maybe, up at the tower house, when we found what we were looking for: a man named Ebenezer. Standing next to him, with a big smile on her face and her arm around his waist, was a woman.

A woman named Gretta.

CHAPTER 11

Could It Be?

"**C**ould this be *our* Gretta?" Trina asked.

"It has to be. I mean, how many Grettas do you know?" Okay, maybe my Ebenezer-being-Jerome theory was kind of nuts, but there was nothing nuts about Gretta *and* Neez.

Trina scanned the caption. "If this *is* our Gretta, her name's Gretta J. Monroe, and if this *is* our Ebenezer, his name is Ebenezer Warner—not 'Varner,' like in the story."

"Warner/Varner—close enough for me. What do you think?"

"I think we should pay ol' Neez a visit. How 'bout you?"

I couldn't have agreed more, so with book in hand yet again, we took off for Neez's office, which we knew was near Mr. Lowell's.

Luckily, Neez was there but, boy-oh-boy, was he surprised to see us again.

"Oh! Hello, kids … didn't expect to see you two again so soon," he said from behind a beat-up old desk. The desk wasn't as fancy as Mr. Lowell's, but it was just as cluttered—in this case with papers and assorted junk, not candlesticks. Neez's office was a jumble of mechanical stuff, like old typewriters and maybe a power tool or two (or a dozen). He was fidgeting with some type of clock when we entered.

"Hey, Neez," I said as breezily as possible, even though

my heart was thumping. Neez seemed like a nice guy, but who knew what would happen when we cornered him with the truth? If it *was* the truth.

"We wanted to show you something," Trina said, placing the book on his desk in front of him.

"Let me get my spectacles," he said with a friendly smile. He reached to a shelf behind him, put on a pair of old-fashioned, wire rimmed glasses, and began to look at the picture.

It was the first time we'd seen Neez with glasses and although the wire rims didn't make him look different (they certainly didn't make him look like Jerome Target), the glasses themselves were familiar. Drumroll please—they looked just like the ones Jerome Target was wearing in his portrait!

We watched for some sort of reaction from Neez as he viewed the photograph in the book, like worry or fear or guilt. What we saw instead was sadness as his face crumpled slightly and his mouth turned down at the corners.

"Is that you?" I asked gently, because he looked like a man who was about to rest his head in his hands, as if the weight of his noggin was too much for his neck to support.

"I knew someone would recognize us eventually," he sighed.

"So it *is* you," Trina said, clapping her hands. "That's you and Gretta, isn't it?"

"Yes, that's me and Gretta. You could say we were sweethearts… a long time ago."

I picked up the book and quickly turned to the page showing Jerome Target. It was hard to see if there was a resemblance between the man in the group photo and the one in the portrait because the faces in the photo were so old and blurred. I turned the book back to him and pointed to Jerome. "Is this you too, then?"

This time Neez looked stricken, like we'd punched him or something. "I told you—Jerome Target died."

Trina nodded. "You also told us that his body was never found, so we figured maybe that's because he didn't really die." Trina said the words like a statement of fact rather than as a question, but either way, the words were begging for Neez to either confirm or deny them.

I tossed my two cents into the mix. "We think that maybe Jerome faked his death, then came back years later to live here again."

Neez looked from me to Trina, then back down at the picture of Jerome Target. My hands began to tingle, and I felt like we were on the verge of a huge discovery. I could see the headline now: *Newsflash! Ebenezer Warner, Caretaker of Mountain Manor House, Is Really Famous Children's Writer Jerome Target!* I decided to push along his tell-all. After all, every good news story needed to answer the five W's.

"I read Jerome Target's story about the sick baby bear and Dr. Ebenezer Varner. Your last name is Warner. You put your own name in the book. Dr. Varner is really you."

"But why did you write under a different name?" Trina questioned. "And why fake your own death?"

"Yeah! And why creep around here at the hotel and not tell anyone who you are … er, were?"

I watched Neez's face closely, and his expression went from surprise to shock to bewilderment, and then to total exhaustion. He looked really tired, like someone had let all the air out of him.

He shook his head slowly. "I know what you kids are thinking, but you have it all wrong. I'm not Jerome Target."

That wasn't exactly the confession I had been anticipating. "You've got to be," I insisted. "Why else would your name end up in one of his stories?"

"That's really not my story to tell," he said, closing the book slowly and pushing it toward us.

I still didn't get it. I had thought we were so close. Now it seemed like we had two mysteries to solve: the location of the missing candlesticks and what really happened to Jerome Target.

Neez didn't totally shut us out, though.

"Look, I think you kids will probably figure this out on your own eventually, but until you do, I'm not at liberty to divulge secrets that were buried a long time ago. I'll be happy to talk to you when you have more information, but that's all I can say for now."

Since Neez wasn't going to spill the beans, and we were out of questions to ask, I picked up the book, thanked Neez for his help, and headed out with Trina.

"Where should we go next?" Trina asked.

"I think the next person on our list should be Gretta," I said.

"Of course!"

We went outside, did some asking around, and learned that Gretta Gershin and her son Henry were in the walled garden. Gretta, it turned out, was an expert at flowers, and Henry was an expert at plants in general. Together, they helped keep the Mountain Manor House fully decorated with flora of all kinds.

The walled garden was west of the lake, so we took a few

meandering paths until we saw the tall, stone walls and the trees and vines growing over the sides.

"This must be it," I said, and we entered through a stone archway.

Now, I don't know much about gardens, but this place truly seemed magical. The trees that we could see above the walls from the outside curved inward, creating a really cool tunnel effect of green leaves. Gravel paths wound this way and that, through squares and circles and rectangles of flower beds filled with all kinds of flowers. I'm no flower expert, so I can't really tell you which kinds they were. I didn't see any daffodils or tulips, but I think I recognized marigolds and roses, plus tons of other colorful sprouters that looked really pretty all grouped together.

We didn't know what Gretta knew about Jerome Target, but there was one thing we knew for certain: she certainly was an expert flower grower.

We wandered up and down the paths, looking for Gretta or even Henry, and we thought we had come across them when we heard voices. Without speaking, Trina and I motioned to each other to be quiet. We crept up to a tall hedge and listened. The voices came through from the other side.

"Someone will find out," said a female voice that sounded very familiar to me.

"Then we'll keep it a secret," said a male voice, which I didn't recognize at all.

"That will be so romantic!" said the female voice again.

Suddenly, I knew who was on the other side of the hedge.

CHAPTER 12

Nowhere to Be Found

I stepped around to the other side of the hedge and sure enough, there she was: My boneheaded sister, Carrie, with some guy I'd never seen before, sitting on a secluded bench surrounded by wildflowers and butterflies.

"I thought you left kinda early this morning," I said when she didn't notice me.

That got her attention.

"Sneak!" she snarled, jumping up from the bench and fisting her hands at her hips. "You followed me!"

Trina joined me just in time. I could tell that Carrie was getting ready to haul off and let loose—not with her fists (she's not the physical type), but with a few verbal swings. "We didn't follow you," Trina said. "We were looking for someone else."

"We have better things to do than spy on you," I added for good measure. Although I was slightly relieved we'd found her, too. I mean, I know she wanted a boyfriend and all, but I also knew Mom and Dad would go bonkers if they found out that their darling daughter was meeting some guy, so I was glad we'd interrupted whatever we'd interrupted. "And do the parents know where you are, by the way?"

"I told them I was going exploring, just like you did," Carrie said with a lift of her chin. "Besides, I don't have to answer to you. Come on, Roy. Let's leave these children and go back to the hotel."

I hadn't taken much notice of Roy so far, but he seemed like a normal, okay guy. He was older than Carrie, but not by much, and he seemed pretty nice and embarrassed, if only just a little. I thought he could be a good "friend" for Carrie for the rest of the week; at least he'd keep her off my back and out of my business.

But I was going to let Mom and Dad know anyway.

Carrie and Roy took off and left me and Trina alone to look for Gretta and Henry, but they weren't in the garden, nor were they in the greenhouse across the hotel property. By this time, it was noon and Trina and I had to leave to eat with our families.

My parents decided not to eat in the dining room this time, but instead to go to the outdoor picnic area, where the hotel people barbecued hot dogs and corn on the cob—picnicky stuff. We sat at a wooden table covered with a red-and-white checkered tablecloth, and swatted at flies and looked at the lake, while a million tall evergreens cast their welcome shade over us.

I was still really caught up with the idea of Neez being Jerome Target. It just made so much sense. I started doodling on a napkin during lunch, trying to tune out Carrie talking on and on about Roy. (I had started that topic of conversation by telling Mom and Dad about my interesting discovery in the garden.) Now that the cat was out of the bag (or Roy, at least), Carrie couldn't keep her mouth shut.

So there I was, writing Jerome's name and Neez's name and Gretta's name, trying to figure out how they all fit together, like wayward pieces in a jigsaw puzzle, when sud–

denly the answer jumped out at me. It literally grabbed my hand and forced my pencil to do the unthinkable.

As I looked down at what I had written, at what my brain had wiggled and jiggled and knocked loose, I felt all the pieces fall into place, even though those pieces also offered up a bunch more questions.

Like why? And how?

I knew my family wouldn't appreciate what I considered to be an amazing revelation, so I kept it to myself. It was difficult though. I wanted to leap up from the picnic table, holler, "Yes! Yes! Yes!" and do a celebration dance.

But that wouldn't have looked very cool, would it? Besides, I didn't want to attract attention.

Instead, I sat through lunch and waited patiently for it to be over, nibbling on an almost-bare corncob and chewing ice cubes from my soda cup. Trina and her family were eating in the dining room, so I couldn't just pass her a note like she had done the day before.

As soon as I was released from lunch, I tore down the path, clambered up the steps that led to the common room, then raced down the hallway to the main dining area.

I saw Trina and her family getting up to leave and waved frantically to get Trina's attention. (Okay, not very cool, I know.) Trina saw me and waved back. Then she pointed me out to her parents, who also waved.

I could barely contain my excitement as Trina fast-walked up to me. "What is it? Did you find Gretta and Henry?"

"Even better." I paused dramatically. "I found Jerome Target!"

CHAPTER 13

Napkin Scribbles

I showed Trina my napkin with all the scribbles, but it didn't make any sense to her. We walked down a short hallway and entered the hotel's gift shop, which also had an old-fashioned ice-cream parlor. After ordering milkshakes at the counter, we sat down at a little round table, and I helped her read my hieroglyphics.

I pulled out a clean napkin and began to write and rip. "Here are the letters of the name *Target*," I said, writing each letter then tearing it out so it was its own little square. "Now rearrange the letters like this"—I moved the letter squares around—"and what does it spell?"

Trina stared at the letters as if she couldn't believe the vision that appeared on the table before her eyes. "Gretta!"

"Right! Now check out the rest of the name. It doesn't fit exactly, but it's pretty close, see?" I proceeded to demonstrate how the letters in *Gretta J. Monroe* formed the name *Jerome Target*, throwing away the extra *o* and *n* in *Monroe*.

"I think the extra letters *n-o* are just to throw people off the track, like, 'No, you're wrong,'" I speculated.

"But I don't get it," Trina said, slurping on her shake, which the girl at the counter had brought over. "How could Gretta be Jerome Target? It doesn't make sense."

"Remember how Mr. Lowell said that people rarely saw

Jerome? That he would write during the day in his room, then go out at night in a big coat and a big hat? Maybe it was really Gretta walking around in disguise."

"But what about the picture? It doesn't look like a woman at all. And if the man in the picture is just some guy from the hotel, someone would have recognized him if he ever showed up at the hotel after Jerome's death. Right?"

The only way to answer her questions and solve the mystery was to ask Gretta herself. But first we had to find her. Between slurps of milkshake, Trina and I discussed where Gretta could possibly be. Then I thought of something that Gretta, Ebenezer, and Jerome Target all had in common— the tower house at the top of the mountain.

"The tower house," I declared loudly. "I bet that's where she is."

Trina removed the straw from her tall milkshake glass and licked the remainder of her shake from the end. "Why the tower house?"

"That's where the picture was taken of Gretta, Neez, and all those other people," I reminded her. "Also, at the end of Jerome Target's stories, the Stillwell family always ends up at the tower house, having a picnic and being really nice to each other and stuff."

Trina placed her straw back in her glass. "Sounds like a plan. Let's go."

We decided to check with my parents first because they had actually hiked up to the tower house the day before. I figured they could direct us to the correct trail, which would save us time in the end.

"Funny you should mention it," Dad said in our hotel room. "Your mother and I were just thinking that it would be a nice family activity to visit the tower house together."

Family activity?

"The hotel has a horse-drawn cart that will take everyone up, so we don't have to hike," Mom informed us. "I believe it leaves within the next half hour."

Well, it wasn't an ideal plan, but the next thing I knew, we were all trooping out to the hotel's main entrance, including Carrie and Roy and Trina's parents and little sister, Sarah, too. I don't know how this had become a family affair, but there we were, all waiting for the horse and cart, when a hotel worker announced that the horse and cart would not be available for the rest of the day.

"The gardening staff has taken the cart to do some work," we were told.

I nudged Trina and said, "The gardening staff? That must be Gretta and Henry. I bet they took the cart up to the tower house."

Trina nudged me right back. "You're right. We've got to get up there."

Trina and I informed our families that we were determined to hike up to the tower house anyway, and a few minutes later we had transformed into a huge hiking party, all winding our way up the side of the mountain, the hotel and the lake below us getting smaller and smaller.

It was a very strange hike, but a lot of fun, too—something that the Stillwell family might have done together. There was a lot of talking and laughing and goofing around, and I almost forgot that Trina and I were actually on a mission—that we actually had a purpose, a reason, for this hike.

But the reason soon came crashing home when we saw the horse and cart outside the tower house.

Now, Trina and I hadn't exactly told our families about the mystery we were trying to solve, let alone our wacky theories. As our families oohed and aahed at the magnificent view from so high up, Trina and I very casually entered the stone tower house. The chilly air within was a drastic change from the warm air outside, and the dim light coming from several small windows overhead barely lit the round space. Therefore, it took a moment for our eyes to adjust to the darkness and for the goosebumps on our skin to subside.

The inside of the tower house wasn't very big—about the size of a small bedroom (if the bedroom was round, that is). On one side of the tower was an iron staircase that led—where else? Up.

I poked my head out the tower house door. "We're going up to the top," I informed our families, who were relaxing on benches set around the perimeter of the tower house and soaking up the sun. Both our parents were too enthralled with Trina's baby sister, Sarah, to take much notice of where we were going, and Carrie and Roy were too into each other to notice that we even existed, so it was no big deal when we took off for a few minutes.

As we climbed the iron staircase that wrapped around the inside of the tower, we heard a distinctly familiar sound coming from the top: voices.

We couldn't make out exactly what was being said, but the voices definitely sounded like older people, like maybe Gretta and Henry. As we crept nearer to the top, the voices got louder and we could make out three people speaking. We continued to tiptoe our way up when suddenly the stairs ended and opened up into a large rooftop room, complete with wide openings that revealed the spectacular view.

Benches were situated against the walls so you could sit there and look out at the scenery.

Who was sitting on one of the benches on the top floor? None other than Gretta and Henry.

And Ebenezer.

"Hi, Henry!" Trina called brightly. "We've been looking everywhere for you to take us on that tour of the gardens."

Well, you should have seen the look of surprise and dismay on the faces of the three adults in that room. They looked like how I must have appeared when Mr. Lowell accused me of stealing the candlesticks—only my expression didn't have guilt mixed in with the surprise and dismay.

"What are you children doing up here?" Gretta scolded. She tried to make her voice sound mean, but it came out quivery, like she was more upset than mad.

"We were just taking a walk with our parents," I answered, going over to a window and waving and calling down to them. It was impossible not to hear their voices down below, shouting up to us.

"Well, we're in the middle of something important here," Gretta continued. "So you two kids can just scram."

Scram? What were we, rats?

"Actually," I replied, "we were looking for you and Henry."

Gretta and her crew remained silent.

"As you know," Trina joined in, "we've been trying to clear Ben here's name and find out who really stole the candlesticks."

"Yeah," I inserted, "and as we were doing that, we found out something very interesting."

Gretta's eyes turned steely and squinty, as if she was trying to assess what we were babbling about; but to her credit, she didn't interrupt us. Yet.

Trina picked up the ball this time. "Uh-huh, very interesting. Want to know what we found out?"

Now it was Henry's turn to speak up. "I'm sure whatever you children discovered has nothing to do with us."

"Um, well, actually, Mr. Gershin, it does," I revealed, dragging it out. "See, at first, we were just trying to clear my name because Gretta had accused me of stealing the candlesticks. But then Neez here got us thinking when he told us that Jerome Target's body was never found."

"Jerome Target," Trina repeated. "The person who wrote in the locked room on the tenth floor. The room where the candlesticks were. Just in case you don't see the connection."

The verbal ball was now in my court. "So we figured that somehow the missing candlesticks and Jerome Target were connected."

"But the only connection we could find was that they both had been in the same room once."

"Then we figured," I went on, "that maybe the reason why Jerome Target's body was never found was because Jerome Target never really died."

"And if he didn't really die *then*," Trina said, "then maybe he's still alive *now* somewhere—somewhere like the Mountain Manor House."

"Stop!" shouted Gretta. "That's enough!"

CHAPTER 14

Open to the Public

Trina and I stared at Gretta as if she'd sprouted an extra nose or something. We had gotten so caught up in trying to catch Gretta or Henry or Neez in a lie that we hadn't paid any attention to how our theories were affecting them. When Gretta had shouted, she'd looked like the mean woman who had hollered at me in Jerome Target's room.

But for all her feistiness, Gretta was still a frail old woman. After her initial outburst, she looked as if someone had removed a steel pole from her spine. She slumped against Neez on the bench and he put his arm around her, as if for support, while Henry patted her knee. Gretta J. Monroe Gershin looked very fragile, like she might shatter at the slightest touch.

"You are Jerome Target, aren't you?" I asked softly.

It felt like forever while Trina and I waited anxiously for her to answer, but finally Gretta heaved a sigh and said, "Yes. I once wrote under the name Jerome Target."

It's funny, but I didn't feel the sense of victory I thought I would. I felt slightly relieved that we had figured it out, but I also felt a little sad. I'm not sure why.

I think Trina must have felt the same way. Her voice was soft when she spoke, not its usual assertive tone. "But why, Mrs. Gershin? Why did you pretend to be dead?"

"Because, dear, Jerome Target *is* dead," she said simply.

"Not to us," I told her. "We read one of the Stillwell stories in school. I'm sure other kids have, too."

Gretta smiled thinly. "That's nice to hear."

Trina was still confused. "I don't get it. Why would you write using a man's name?"

Gretta sat back and leaned against the wall. Trina and I made ourselves comfortable on one of the empty benches that surrounded the tower room's uppermost floor.

"Things were different back then," Gretta began. "The last thing my family wanted me to do was become a writer. They wanted me to marry a nice man, settle down, and have children. But I wasn't ready for that, so I came to the Mountain Manor House one summer to clear my head."

"And you met Ebenezer," I said.

Gretta's smile grew slightly and she looked at Neez. "Yes, I did. We had such a lovely time here those few months."

"Then what happened?" Trina encouraged.

Gretta folded her hands in her lap and studied them. She spoke slowly. "When the summer ended, everyone returned to their families, but I still wasn't ready to face mine. My family had sent for me and had enclosed a letter from my intended husband, Xavier Gershin. I knew my time here was almost over, but I didn't want it to end. I begged them for a few more months, and I rented the room on the tenth floor."

"Where you created Jerome Target," I filled in.

"Yes," Gretta said. "I wanted to write about the wonderful times I had had here at the Mountain House so I would never forget, and I wanted others to discover how magnificent the Mountain House was, too. I knew it was difficult for women to be published, so I chose a pen name."

"You switched around some of the letters of your own name," Trina said. "Ben figured it out this afternoon."

I shrugged like it was no big deal. "I was just doodling and realized that *Gretta* has the same letters as *Target*."

"Clever boy," Gretta said with a slight glint in her eye. "I wrote by day, and at night I went out, disguised as a man."

"And the portrait?" Trina asked.

Gretta and Neez looked at each other and chuckled. "Neez helped me set that up. If you look closely, that's really me underneath Neez's glasses and inside his suit."

"Really?" I was impressed.

"Really."

We were quiet for a moment. I knew the question that had to be asked next, but it was a tough one.

Finally, I said, "But why did you kill yourself? Well, not yourself, but, well, you know."

"Yes, indeed I do." Gretta sighed and looked at Neez. He nodded as if telling her it was okay, and she continued. "I knew that Jerome Target couldn't continue to write—*I* couldn't continue to write. My parents were insistent that I marry Xavier, and he was a good man," she said, touching Henry on the arm. "So Neez and I decided that Jerome Target had to die, and he helped me fake Jerome's death."

"But where did you go after?" I said, baffled.

"Neez helped me get down the mountain, and I returned to my family. I married Xavier a few months later, and then a year after that, Henry was born."

Trina turned to Henry. "Did you know about this?"

Henry cleared his throat. "Well, er, yes, I did. But not until after my father died. We visited the hotel to help come to grips with his passing, and while we were here, Mother told me all about her summer. Like you, I figured out that she was Jerome Target. I took one look at the portrait on the tenth floor, and I knew it was Mother."

Then it dawned on me. "So that's why the room is kept locked. You're afraid someone will recognize you."

"It's something that has always worried me, yes," Gretta said. "As the years went by, I knew the chances of being discovered had become slimmer and slimmer, but it was an old habit that was hard to break."

"So you stole the candlesticks, right?" Trina asked.

Gretta looked sheepish, but she nodded. "It was a terrible thing to do, to blame you, Ben. But when I saw you children in the room, I was afraid that you would steal some of Jerome's—I mean my—things. I wanted the candlesticks to be safe. Then when Patrice found me in the room, I panicked. Being so close to Jerome's portrait, I acted irrationally. My old fears of being recognized took over. I accused Patrice of stealing the candlesticks to distract her from looking too closely at me or the painting."

"And Henry was in there, too, right?" I added. "That's why the door was unlocked. But then Henry went out on the balcony when he heard me come in."

"You children are very smart," Gretta said. "Very smart."

Trina turned to Neez. "Neez, why did you help Gretta if you knew she was going to marry someone else? Didn't that, like, I don't know, hurt or something?"

Neez smiled sadly and looked at Gretta, then back at us. "It sure did. In fact, I never married because I never stopped loving Gretta. Every summer I came back, hoping she'd return as well. One summer, twenty years later, she did."

He smiled broadly and Gretta returned his smile.

"I was always very proud of Gretta's writing," Neez continued, "and it was difficult for me to pretend not to know who Jerome Target really was. I suppose that's why I dropped the clue about Jerome Target's body never having been found. After all these years, I think that, subconsciously, I wanted the truth to be known. I wanted Gretta to finally get the credit I so firmly believe she deserves."

I thought I saw a tear or two in both their eyes.

Just then, my dad poked his head up from the stairwell. "Here you two are!" he said. Then he frowned when he saw Gretta, remembering how she had accused me at dinner that first night. It seemed like eons ago!

Before he could say anything hurtful to Gretta, I spoke up. "Dad, uh, this is Gretta Gershin and her son Henry, and this is Ebenezer Warner. We found the candlesticks and everything's okay now, but it's a long story, so we'll tell you all about it on the way down the mountain." I spoke quickly, jumbling all my thoughts and sentences together before Dad had a chance to interrupt. I knew if he started asking questions, the answers would get all confused.

Gretta stood up and leaned on her walking stick. "Would you all like a ride back down in the horse cart?"

Dad still wasn't too sure what to make of it all, but he agreed, and we made our way down the stairs, stepping carefully so we didn't go tumbling down like a row of dominoes.

Once out in the sunshine, Trina and I made introductions all around. Then we all clambered aboard the cart and Henry told the horse to "Giddy-ap!" Trina and I explained how we found the candlesticks, who Jerome Target was, and how we figured out that Gretta was really Jerome Target. The next thing I knew, we were convincing Gretta that she had to tell Mr. Lowell her secret identity and that the room on the tenth floor should be opened to the public.

Surprisingly, we got Gretta to agree. Maybe it was because she had held the secret in for so long and now it was pleading with her conscience to be revealed to everyone else. Maybe it was because she finally wanted people to know that she was Jerome Target and that he was still alive.

Or maybe it was because it was just time. Time to say goodbye to that summer so long ago and to embrace the summers that she and Neez and Henry still had ahead.

I'm sounding very philosophical, I know.

For the rest of the week, Trina and I helped Gretta, Neez, and Henry get the room on the tenth floor ready for visitors. We polished the furniture and dusted the books. We set out old pictures of Gretta and Neez. We blew up a picture of a young Gretta and placed it next to the portrait of Jerome Target. If you looked closely, you could see that Jerome/Gretta was smiling a secret smile.

I also did a lot of family bonding with Mom, Dad, and yes, even Carrie—just like my parents had hoped. We hiked a few more trails, drove into the local town for antiques, and even picnicked at the tower house—just like Gretta's Stillwell Family often did. Sometimes Roy came along, but usually it was just the four of us.

Carrie said a tearful goodbye to her new friend, and I wondered if they'd remember each other the way Neez and Gretta never forgot their summer so long ago.

Trina and I exchanged addresses and e-mails, and we promised that we'd keep in touch.

You know what else? That whole week, I completely forgot that we didn't have a TV.